The Mask

Written by Sally Pollack

STECK-VAUGHN
COMPANY
ELEMENTARY • SECONDARY • ADULT • LIBRARY

Get one round paper plate.
Get some colored paper.

Add two triangles for ears.

 3

Add two ovals for eyes.

Add one round ball of cotton for a nose.

 5

Add one square and two triangles for a mouth.

Add six thin rectangles beside the nose.

 7

Meow!